1 3 5 7 9 10 8 6 4 2

Copyright © John Prater 1999

John Prater has asserted his right under the
Copyright, Designs and Patents Act, 1988,
to be identified as the author of this work

First published in the United Kingdom 1999
by The Bodley Head Children's Books
Random House, 20 Vauxhall Bridge Road, London SW1V 2SA

Random House Australia (Pty) Limited
20 Alfred Street, Milsons Point, Sydney
New South Wales 2061, Australia

Random House New Zealand Limited
18 Poland Road, Glenfield
Auckland 10, New Zealand

Random House South Africa (Pty) Limited
Endulini, 5A Jubilee Road,
Parktown 2193, South Africa

Random House UK Limited Reg. No. 954009

A CIP catalogue record for this book
is available from the British Library

ISBN 0 370 32368 8

Printed in Singapore

The Bear Went Over the Mountain

by John Prater

THE BODLEY HEAD
LONDON

The bear went

over the mountain...

The bear went

over the mountain...

The bear went

over the mountain...

To see what

he could see.

And the other side

of the mountain...

The other side

of the mountain...

The other side

of the mountain...

Was all that

he could see.

So he went back

over the mountain...

He went back

over the mountain...

He went back

over the mountain...

So very

happily.